The House of Lazarus

by

James Lovegrove

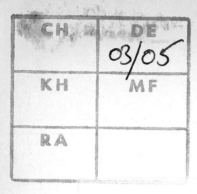

Published in 2003 in Great Britain by
Barrington Stoke Ltd
10 Belford Terrace, Edinburgh EH4 3DQ
First published in different form in *Destination Unknown*
(Borealis, an imprint of White Wolf Publishing,
Stone Mountain, Georgia, USA, 1997)

ISBN 1-842991-25-6

Printed by Polestar Wheatons Limited

A Note from the Author

What if you could escape death? What if you could buy yourself a form of eternal life, but at a very steep price? Would you be prepared to pay that price, or have someone who loves you pay it for you?

That's the idea behind *The House of Lazarus.** It's a story set in the near future, perhaps 15 or 20 years from now. Science is a little more advanced, but basically the world in this book is much the same as our world.

Thanks to science, people in this future can be kept on the brink of death for ever. But it's an expensive business. And is it really worthwhile keeping them alive in this way? Who benefits more? The dead people themselves, or the people who love them and live on after them?

The story's hero, Joey Newman, sets out to answer these questions for himself. I hope that the discoveries he makes will surprise you ... and make you think.

*Gordon Lazarus is the name of the founder of the firm. Lazarus was also someone in the Bible who was raised from the dead.

Contents

Chapter 1
Stack 339, Drawer 41

You were welcome at the House of Lazarus at any time. But it was cheaper to come at night, when you could get an off-peak rate. Also, the building was less busy then. During the day it was full of people, and noisy. At night you could have a bit more peace and privacy with your loved one.

The receptionist in the entrance hall thought it was odd that Joey came in wearing sunglasses. It was dark outside, and just a short while ago it had been raining.

She smiled at him anyway, as though they were old friends. She didn't use his name, however, until after Joey had said he was there to visit his mother, Mrs Barbara Newman.

The receptionist looked up the name Newman on her desktop computer terminal and saw that Mrs Barbara Newman had a son called Joey.

"It's Joey, isn't it?" the receptionist said. She was only about three years older than him. She smiled again. "We haven't seen you here for a couple of weeks."

"I've been busy," said Joey. He was, in fact, more than "busy". He had just started an evening job at a bar on Bay Street, on top of his day job selling insurance at the call centre. But he didn't think the receptionist was interested in hearing about that. More to the point, he was tired and irritable and he couldn't be bothered to make small talk.

The receptionist folded her hands and placed them on her desktop, which was a long, broad slab of white marble.

"It's not my place to tell you what to do, Joey," she said. "But you are Mrs Newman's only living relative. And we do like our residents to be stimulated as much as possible. As you know, we wake them for an hour every morning and an hour every evening. In the morning, we broadcast news to them. In the evening, we play them a programme of easy-listening music.

"But it's much more useful to have someone come in and talk to them. Think of it as 'mental P.E.'. Conversation keeps their minds fit and healthy."

"I visit whenever I can," said Joey.

"Of course you do. Of course you do." The receptionist continued to smile. It was the sort of smile that said Joey didn't need to apologise. She forgave him. "This isn't a complaint," she added. "I'm just making a suggestion."

"Well, thank you for the suggestion."

Joey gave her his credit card.
The receptionist swiped it through a reader and handed it back. Then she pressed a button on a panel set into the desktop.

A man came out from a nearby doorway. He was wearing a crisp, white outfit like a male nurse's uniform – a buttoned white tunic, white trousers, white shoes. He was one of the orderlies who assisted visitors at the House of Lazarus.

"Barbara Newman," the receptionist told the orderly. "Stack 339, Drawer 41."

"This way, sir." The orderly beckoned to Joey and led him over to a pair of large doors. There was a panel of beaten copper set into the wall next to the doors. The picture on it showed a man and a woman who looked as if they were fast asleep. They were lying on their backs with their arms by their sides and their eyes closed. They looked very peaceful. There were electrodes attached to them at the forehead, chest and leg.

There was a sudden drop in temperature as Joey and the orderly passed through the doors and entered the next room. Cold air fell over Joey's face like an icy veil. Goose bumps prickled on his skin. He craned his neck to look up.

The Wall always amazed him, no matter how many times he came to the House of Lazarus. It was at least 50 metres high and nearly two kilometres long. It curved away to the left and the right. It was like a vast, gleaming cliff. Arc lamps shot beams of intense white light down it. The ceiling above it was arched like the ceiling of a cathedral.

The Wall was made up of stacks of steel drawers, each a little larger than a coffin. The stacks began about two metres above the floor and rose all the way up to the ceiling. There were a thousand stacks and fifty thousand drawers in total. Sometimes Joey found it hard to believe that every one of the drawers contained a human being.
A not-quite-dead human being.

Comfortable leather armchairs were arranged at the foot of the Wall. The armchairs were lined up in rows like pews in a church. There were people sitting in them here and there, murmuring softly. Every so often someone might nod or move a hand, but a lot of the time the people just sat in silence with their heads bent on one side, listening.

In the background there was the soft hum of machinery. This was the sound of thousands of cryogenic units all whirring and whispering at once.

The orderly walked down an aisle between two rows of armchairs, then turned left at the end. Joey followed him. The orderly's shoes had rubber soles that made a soft, squelching noise. Joey wore boots with heels that clacked loudly.

The orderly and Joey moved along the base of the Wall until they came to Stack number 339. The orderly turned to Joey and indicated that he should sit down in a nearby chair. Then he began tapping commands into a small, hand-held computer.

Joey sat in the chair and took off his sunglasses. He folded them up and slipped them into his shirt pocket. The orderly caught sight of the dark purple rings beneath Joey's eyes and frowned. It looked as if someone had punched Joey, giving him two black eyes.

But the purple rings were there simply because he was worn out. They were the result of all the hours Joey spent working, the long days and late nights.

The orderly looked back at his computer. "Right," he said. "I've given your mother a wake-up call. Put on your headset."

Joey did as he was told. Each chair had a headset that was connected by a wire to a panel in one of the armrests. There were two buttons on the panel, a red one and a blue one. There was also a dial that controlled the volume. The headset was made of thin, black metal and was very light. Joey fitted it onto his head. An earpiece went over his ear. A microphone hung beside his mouth.

"Can you hear anything?" the orderly asked.

Joey shook his head.

"She may take a moment or two to wake up. Press the red button if you need me for

8

any reason. Press the blue button when you're finished. That'll disconnect you. OK?"

Joey stifled a yawn. Not only was he tired but he knew these instructions as well as the orderly did.

"Have a nice chat." The orderly turned and left, squelching along to a door set into the Wall. The door was marked STAFF ONLY and could be opened by tapping a five-digit code number into a keypad. It hissed slowly shut behind the orderly.

Joey sat and waited. His gaze was fixed on one of the drawers near the top of Stack 339. Drawer number 41.

That was where his mother lay.

Chapter 2

A Conversation with the Dead

The first sounds that came through the headset were dim and soft. They seemed to come from somewhere deep in the ocean, where whales wail and the mouths of drowned sailors drift open and shut with the tides. They seemed to belong to another world.

Joey heard them in the earpiece. The sounds murmured and burbled and groaned, growing louder. They became sharper and clearer. He heard little snippets of speech, fragments of a familiar voice. All at once, he was listening to his mother.

"Hello? Who's that? Is there someone there?" she was saying.

His mother sounded confused, the way older people do when they have just woken up.

She spoke again. "Hello? Hello? Oh dear. I'm sure there's someone there. Who is it? Who am I talking to?"

"Hi, Mum," said Joey. "It's me."

"Joey! Oh, Joey. How nice of you to drop by. It's so good to hear your voice. It's been a while since we last talked, hasn't it?"

"Just three days, Mum."

"Three days? It feels an awful lot longer than that. But then it's so easy to lose track of time in here. Well, anyway. How are you?"

"I'm fine. And you?"

"I must be all right, I suppose. Nothing changes in here, so I must be staying the same. Are you *quite* sure it's only been three days? I try and keep a count of the number of times they wake me. The news. And that dreadful tinkly-plonk music they play. Like the stuff you hear when you're in a lift."

"OK, maybe not three days. A few days," Joey admitted.

"You don't need to lie to me, Joey."

"I've been meaning to come more often, Mum. But it's not easy, what with one thing and another."

"It's all right, love. I do understand. There are plenty of things more important than your old mother. Plenty of things. How's work?"

"OK. Same as usual," said Joey.

"It's not a job for a bright boy like you. A university graduate, working as an insurance salesman. What a waste of your talents."

"It's the best I could get, Mum. I'm lucky to have a job at all."

"And have you found yourself a nice girl yet?" asked his mother.

"Not yet." Joey sounded angry.

"Don't take it like that, Joey. I'm only asking. You don't have to tell me. I only want to know if you're happy."

"I'm happy, Mum," replied Joey.

"Well, that's good, then. And the flat? Have you had the cockroach problem sorted out?"

"I rang the council yesterday. They said they'd send a pest control man round to deal with it, but he never turned up. I think he may have been mugged on the way."

Muggings happened often in the Dock District, where Joey lived. It wasn't a safe area. Not long ago, a gang of local teenagers had attacked the men who came round to collect the rubbish. They had held up the rubbish collectors at knifepoint and stolen their lorry.

It was hard to understand why anyone would want a lorry full of other people's old rubbish, but that was what life was like in the Dock District.

Joey's mother was really waking up now.

"By now, love, you ought to have moved to somewhere else," she said. "Can't you afford somewhere a bit nicer, even with a job like yours? There's lots of property being built. I heard it on the news. Shiny, new tower blocks are popping up all over the city like mushrooms. And yet you insist on staying where you are."

"I like it there," Joey told her.

"Well, *I* don't like the idea of you being there." His mother sounded distressed.

"Anyway, I can't afford to live somewhere else. I don't have the money for a deposit on the rent."

"Oh, rot! What about your father's money?"

"Mum, it's not as simple as that."

"It seems perfectly simple to me."

"Well, it would, wouldn't it?" Joey was aware of raising his voice. His words echoed up to the high ceiling of the House of Lazarus. He imagined his mother, cooped up inside Drawer 41. To her, it must have sounded like he was bellowing.

"And what's that remark supposed to mean?" she said.

"Nothing, Mum," he said, more quietly. "Nothing at all. I'm sorry."

His mother's feelings were hurt. "What is it, Joey? What's wrong with you? We always start out chatting so nicely, and then I go and say something, I don't know what, but *something*, and all of a sudden you're shouting at me. I never know what it is I've said that's wrong. I wish you'd tell me, Joey. I wish you'd tell me what it is I do that makes you so angry."

"It's nothing, Mum, honest. Look, I've had a long day, that's all. I get a little snappish sometimes when I'm tired."

He decided not to tell her about the bar job. She would only worry that he was taking on too much work. She would also think that he should not be working in a smoky, seedy bar.

It was bad enough that he spent all day on the phone at the call centre. She had always felt that he should be doing something better with his life. She would be even more upset

17

if she learned that he now had two badly paid jobs, instead of just one.

"Yes, well," she said, "I'm sorry, too. But you must understand, it gets very lonely in here. Very, very lonely. It's just me in the dark, and you're my lifeline to the world, Joey. You're the only person who comes to visit me. If you didn't come, I don't know what I'd do. Go mad, probably. As soon as you leave, I look forward to the next time we can talk."

"I won't leave it so long next time, Mum."

"That's the best I can hope for, I suppose. Off you go then, love. Thanks for dropping by. It was lovely chatting. Come back when you can." She gave a little laugh. "I'm not going anywhere!"

"All right, Mum. Take care."

"Bless you, Joey."

"Goodnight, Mum. Sleep tight."

Joey removed the headset and pushed the blue button which broke the connection between them. He sat for a while, listening to the hum from the electric tombs in which fifty thousand men, women and children lay slumbering. His skin tingled with the chill that came from the Wall of steel drawers. He got up to go.

The orderly arrived with his hand-held computer to shut down Joey's mother's brain and send her back to sleep.

Chapter 3

Keeping the Memories Alive

In the entrance hall, the receptionist presented Joey with a bill to sign. "I've added the rent for this month," she said. "It's due in a couple of days. I thought you wouldn't mind."

Joey did mind. He blinked as he looked at the figure at the bottom of the bill. It hurt.

"I don't have enough left on my credit card to pay for all this," he said. "I can cover the conversation I've just had. I just don't think I can pay the rent right now as well."

The receptionist's smile became a fraction less friendly. "That's fine," she said. "I thought it would be simpler for you to pay it all in one go. You do, of course, have a month to come up with the rent. And I don't need to remind you that, if you fail to settle the account by then, your contract with us will end and we will take steps to shut down your mother."

"I know." Joey handed the bill back to her.

The receptionist ripped up the bill and printed off a new one, which charged only for the conversation with his mother. Joey wrote his signature at the bottom.

"How is she?" the receptionist asked.

"The same," Joey said. "The same as she always is."

He went outside.

The bus stop was a short walk down the road from the House of Lazarus. Joey waited there for half an hour, shivering in the damp, night wind. At least it hadn't started raining again.

Finally a bus came.

On board, Joey sat with his head against the window and watched the city slide past.

He saw blackened walls covered with graffiti which looked like an alien language written in spray paint. He saw small areas of park which no-one dared go into after dark. He saw shops with thick, steel shutters over their windows. He saw neon signs reflected in puddles as wriggling streaks, like Day-Glo snakes. He saw people walking on the pavements with their heads down, their hands buried in their pockets.

He saw police cars cruising by. The police officers kept their eyes straight ahead. They didn't look around at all.

****

Joey remembered how his mother had been in the hospital, when she was very ill with cancer.

He remembered her saying, "I don't want to die, Joey."

Her voice was small and frightened. Her lips were pale grey. Her skull showed beneath the skin of her face. Her eyes seemed too big for their sockets.

"I'm so scared, Joey."

It was hard for her to talk. Every word was an effort. She gasped and gurgled like a blocked drain whenever she took a breath.

He remembered the way her hair looked. The radiation treatment for her cancer had left her with just a few wispy tufts. Her hair surrounded her head like a thin halo.

He remembered how her arms were like sticks. The veins stood out on them, wrapped around the bones like twisting vines.

He remembered how painful it was for her to turn her head to look at him. It was a slow, agonising movement that seemed to take hours.

****

Joey's thoughts were interrupted by a man in a nearby seat on the bus who had begun to cheer. The man was watching a game show on the TV screen that was set into the headrest of the seat in front of him. Every seat in the bus was fitted with one of these TV screens. They played to you whether you wanted to watch them or not.

On the game show, the audience was clapping madly. A contestant had just answered a question and won herself a fortnight's holiday on a tropical island.

The man on the bus was delighted by the contestant's success. He was pink in the face and clearly very drunk. "Well done," he said to the contestant.

Joey turned his head to look out at the city again. His thoughts returned to his mother.

****

Her hospital room was so bright. The light was harsh. It didn't allow anything to hide. It wiped out all the shadows.

"There are ways, Joey," his mother said. "I don't *have* to die."

Her hand lay limply on the bed. He reached out and took hold of it. In the

26

past it had always been the other way round. His mother was the one who would touch him, holding his arm or kissing his cheek. Joey was never the one to reach across the space between them and make contact.

She tried to squeeze his fingers. She had so little strength left in her that Joey barely felt a thing. "We can afford it," she said.

A salesman from the House of Lazarus had visited the hospital earlier that week. He had spoken to many of the patients and their relatives, and had left brochures in all of the wards that were for people who were dying.

There was a brochure on the little cabinet next to Joey's mother's bed. Joey could tell she had read through it several times, because the corners of the pages were crumpled and dog-eared. She had also pulled out the application form that came bound in with the brochure. She had filled in many of the boxes on the form, although she had left some of them blank. Her handwriting was a faint scrawl, very difficult to read.

****

Back on the bus, the drunk man was getting even more excited.

"No!" he shouted. The contestant on the game show had just given the wrong answer to a question.

"I'm sorry but that's the wrong answer, Margaret," the game show host told her. He didn't sound sorry at all.

The drunk man knew the right answer. "*Steamboat Willie*," he yelled. "That was the first cartoon Mickey Mouse appeared in."

"The correct answer, Margaret, is *Steamboat Willie*," the game show host went on.

"Yeah!" said the drunk man. "That's what I said. Stupid woman."

"All right," said the host. "That's the last of your three 'lives' gone. This is the final question. Get this one right, Margaret, and you'll keep all the prizes you've won so far, including the tropical holiday and the luxury home. Get it wrong ... and you'll lose everything."

The host waved his hand as he spoke the last two words, and the audience chanted them along with him. It was the title of the game show: *Lose Everything*.

"Lose everything," mumbled the drunk man. "Yeah."

Joey closed his eyes to shut out the drunk man and his game show.

****

His mother's face was as white as the pillows she lay on.

"We've still got enough money in the bank," she said. "I know the hospital bills

29

have been steep, but still. We've more than enough money. I'm sure of it."

It was all so simple to her. Her life was seeping away. Her organs were failing one by one. The doctors had given her less than a month to live. She didn't want to die, and the brochure from the House of Lazarus told her that she didn't have to die.

"All you need to do is complete the form and give your consent," she said. "It's what your father would have wanted," she added.

Joey's father had died in a train crash when Joey was very young. Joey could barely remember him. He could recall big, broad hands and a clean smell of aftershave. Apart from that, all he knew about his father were things his mother had told him.

The train company had admitted responsibility for the crash. It had paid out large sums in compensation to the relatives of the victims who had died. Joey and his mother had used some of the money to live on. They had used some more of it so that Joey could go to university. But there was still quite a lot of it left. Or that was what Joey's mother thought.

"I can't do it without your signature," his mother said. "They have to have the consent of a close relative."

Joey should have said something to her then. Why hadn't he? Why had he kept his mouth shut? Maybe he hadn't wanted to let her down, that was all.

****

"But you're going to have to wait a moment, Margaret," said the game show host. He turned to the camera. His teeth shone. "We're going to take a commercial break right now. Stay with us to see if Margaret will go all the way and win tonight's star prize, plus all the prizes she's collected so far, or if she'll ... *lose everything*."

The audience cheered. The game show's theme tune jingled jauntily. The drunk man tump-ti-tummed along.

The first of the commercials was one for the House of Lazarus.

Joey looked at the screen in front of him.

The commercial began in an office.

There was a marble bust of some Roman emperor. There was a painting set in a fancy, gold frame, a dark landscape from the eighteenth century. There was a large desk made of walnut wood.

Gordon Lazarus himself sat on a corner of the desk. He wore a coal-black suit. His hair was ash-grey and smoothly combed. His head was bent forwards. His arms were folded loosely. He looked like someone who really, truly *cared*.

"There comes a time when each of us must say goodbye to someone we love," Lazarus said. "For many, it is the most painful thing they will ever have to do."

The camera glided in towards him.

"But what if you could be spared that pain? What if you were able to stay in touch with your loved ones even after they had been taken from you?"

His lips curved into a gentle smile. Lazarus's teeth weren't quite as shiny as the game show host's.

Then the commercial cut to a shot of the Wall. The camera swept slowly across the fronts of the fifty thousand steel drawers.

Lazarus was still speaking, even though for the moment he was no longer visible. "Here, at the House of Lazarus, we have done years of research into the science of cryogenics. We have developed remarkable new methods for preserving living tissue. All this hard work has led us to one result. A breathtaking result. We can now delay the actual moment of death for ever."

The camera continued its sweep and found Lazarus standing at the foot of the Wall. Some of the leather armchairs could be seen just in the corner of the picture. People were sitting in them with the headsets on, chatting away. They were actors, and they looked relaxed and happy.

"Before now, you would have to go to a medium to get in touch with your loved ones. The medium would channel what they were saying," said Lazarus. "But we have developed a better way. At the House of Lazarus we keep your loved ones suspended between life and death.

"We store them at subzero temperatures and hold them just this side of clinical death. We stimulate the nerve endings in their brains and use electronic devices to convert their brain impulses into speech. This means your loved ones can talk with you long after the breath has left their bodies. Though on the brink of death, they are not gone. Though lost, they live on."

Lazarus smiled again. "Call our freephone number to find out more, or visit our website."

He spread out his arms as if to say, *It's that simple.*

"The House of Lazarus," he said. "Where death is not the end."

Some words slowly formed on the screen:

THE HOUSE OF LAZARUS

KEEPING THE MEMORIES ALIVE

"Poor bastards," said the drunk man. "Let 'em rest in peace, that's what I say."

****

On his next visit to the hospital, Joey brought back the brochure, which he had taken home with him. He had studied the application form and had filled out the parts which his mother had left blank. Now, back at the hospital, he and his mother had a meeting with the salesman from the House of Lazarus.

"She's right to be doing this," the salesman said. He took the form off Joey and folded it in half with a satisfied look on his face.

Joey's eyes filled with tears.

"We'll see to it that everything is in place," the salesman said to him. "It's vital that we are present at your mother's final moment. There is a brief window of opportunity between physical death and brain

death. That's when we take action. One of
our recovery teams will be on stand by,
waiting for the call from the hospital.
I'll make all the arrangements."

"OK," Joey said. He felt numb.

"Before that, we'll need to run a few tests.
We'll need to take tissue samples from your
mother. We'll need to do some interviews, so
that we can sample her speech patterns."
The salesman raised his eyebrows. "And then
there is the matter of payment."

Joey's mother struggled to turn her face
to look at Joey. Her eyes begged him to tell
her that everything was all right.

Did she know? Joey still wasn't sure, even
now. Did she know that there had been
almost nothing left of the compensation
money from the train company? The hospital
fees had been enormous. And Joey was going
to have to pay a huge amount in death duties

when she died. What was left after that would hardly cover the first year's rent at the House of Lazarus, and Joey would have to use his own money to pay for any future conversations he had with her.

Joey wanted to believe that his mother had not known any of this. She had been too ill to work it out. Her cancer had gone on a long time and her suffering had stopped her from thinking about things too clearly.

****

Meanwhile, on the bus, the drunk man was snoring. It was so loud that Joey almost missed the announcement over the loudspeaker.

"Next stop the Dock District," the driver said. "Change at the Dock District for Eastport, the Satellite Islands and Coastal Drive."

No-one except Joey got off the bus.

Chapter 4
Grave Robbing

Joey was almost too tired to undress when he got home. He managed to get all his clothes off except his underpants. Then he slumped down onto the bed face-first.
He reached up to switch off the bedside lamp. Sleep came over him like every curtain in the world closing at once.

At some point during the night, Joey had a dream.

****

Joey dreamed he was standing over his mother's grave. It was a traditional grave in a traditional cemetery. The headstone was a slab of black granite carved with the name BARBARA NEWMAN. Beneath that were the dates which marked the beginning and end of her life, like bookends. There was also an inscription:

A GOOD MOTHER

LOVED BY HER SON

No grass had grown over the grave yet. It was covered by a shallow mound of soil. Joey prodded the soil with his foot and it gave way softly. Fresh, brown grit spilled around the toes of his boots. He realised that his mother must have been buried within the past 24 hours. He didn't think there was anything strange about this at all. He even thought he might remember a funeral service.

The cemetery was crowded with graves and tombs. It was surrounded by trees with no leaves on their branches. The sun was bright and wintry. Joey was alone.

The body of his mother lay beneath the ground in front of him, less than two metres down. He found it difficult to believe that she could be so close, but also so far away.

(Perhaps some small corner of his brain was reminding him that his mother was not buried here after all. Her body was lying somewhere else. It was halfway across the city, at the House of Lazarus.)

In his dream, he thought that he could reach down and touch his mother's face if he wanted to. All that lay between him and her was a little bit of earth and a coffin lid.

For some reason, this made him quite angry. It seemed absurd to stick dead people

under the ground but still so close to the surface. It was a way of torturing the people who were still alive and still grieving.
The dead should be thrown into bottomless pits. They should be put somewhere where they would disappear for ever and be forgotten. They shouldn't be put in a place where anyone could dig them up again easily.

Joey fell to his knees and started digging.

He scooped at the earth with his hands. He shovelled the dirt aside. He worked like a dog trying to get at a buried bone.

He reached the lid of his mother's coffin with surprising speed. The coffin wasn't even two metres down as it was supposed to be. It was only a few centimetres down.

He cleared all the dirt from the lid. Suddenly the lid was shiny and clean, as if the coffin had not even been buried. Six wing nuts held the lid in place. They were made of brass and gleamed in the cold sunshine.

Joey unscrewed them swiftly, throwing each one over his shoulder as it came free. As the last wing nut came undone, the coffin lid gave a little jump. The coffin wanted to be opened, it seemed.

Joey hesitated. He was seconds away from seeing his mother's face again. It occurred to him that she might not be a pretty sight. Decay would have gone to work on her body, even after just a short time. Did he really want to look at her when she was like that? Did he really want to see her all purple and bloated?

But no – he had to see her. He had to see her body with his own eyes. He had to know that she was there in the coffin, lifeless and gone.

He wedged his fingers beneath the lid and levered it up. It looked heavy but in fact it wasn't. It weighed so little that it could have been made of cardboard. He flipped it off easily. The lid landed upside down on the grass next to the grave and lay there, rocking gently from side to side.

Now everything in the dream seemed to happen in slow motion.

It took Joey ages to look away from the upturned lid and move his gaze over to the open coffin. He was worried that he was going to wake up before he had a chance to look into the coffin. His dreams often ended without reaching a proper conclusion. It was like walking out of the cinema five minutes before the film finished.

He became more worried, because, in his other dreams, he had always woken up once he started to think about waking up. He made himself look towards the coffin. He forced himself to look inside.

****

And then he was awake. There was daylight beneath the bedroom curtains.

44

The alarm clock beside his bed said it was nearly six o'clock. At six the alarm clock would start beeping.

Joey shook his head. The last moments of the dream lingered in his memory.

The coffin had been empty. He had known all along that it would be. What else had he expected? His mother wasn't buried in a cemetery. She was lying in a steel drawer at the House of Lazarus.

Sometimes he did have the most stupid dreams!

Chapter 5
The Empty Coffin

But Joey wasn't able to forget about the dream. Nor could he ignore it.

All day long he sat in front of his computer screen at the call centre. He went through the telephone directory. His job was to call total strangers and ask them if they had ever thought about household insurance, life insurance, car insurance, pet insurance. Were they happy with their current insurance policies? Were they interested in getting a better deal?

Some people were rude to him. Some pretended they were listening but then put the phone down without warning. Some *were* interested and wanted to hear more. But only a few of these ended up buying an insurance policy from Joey, and earning him some money on commission.

He was used to all that. It didn't bother him.

What bothered him was the last thing he had seen in the dream before waking up.

The coffin gaped up at him, empty. Its red satin lining was clean and unmarked. It showed that his mother had never been lying there.

And he just couldn't shake this image from his head. It was strange and scary. It seemed to mock him. It was even a sort of insult.

He was still thinking about the dream as he worked at the bar on Bay Street that evening. The only time it wasn't on his mind was during Happy Hour. That was when the drinks were cheap and the bar was packed with customers. Joey had to rush around to make sure everyone got what they ordered. He couldn't think about much else then, except doing his job properly.

When things were a bit less busy, he mentioned the dream to Rita, who was the manageress of the bar. Rita was interested in horoscopes and fortune-telling and the meaning of dreams and stuff like that. Her face took on a wise expression as he described the cemetery and the mound of soil and the open coffin.

"It's all about not being sure of anything any more," she told him. "The empty coffin represents how lonely you are without your mother. The red lining is your pain and grief. You still haven't come to terms with those. You dug her up, which means you want to try and bring your troubles to the surface. You want to try and face them. But it's very difficult to do so."

Rita did not know that Joey's mother was at the House of Lazarus. Joey did not like to tell anyone about that. Normally, it was only rich people who could afford the fees at the House of Lazarus, and Joey was not rich.

It was easier to pretend to people that his mother was just plain dead. It avoided awkward questions. The lie was simpler than the truth.

Rita patted him on the back. "Does that help?"

"Yes," Joey said. "It does. Thanks."

But it didn't help. Not one bit.

The trouble was that Joey didn't feel love for his mother any longer. He felt the same way about her as he felt about the coffin in the dream. It was empty and so was she, and this appalled him. He hated her for what she was putting him through.

He detested having to work so hard to keep her in the drawer at the House of Lazarus. He resented having to go there and talk to her. He felt as if she had cheated him somehow. He wasn't able to go on with his life, because she had insisted on going on with *her* life.

He realised that perhaps things would have been different, if only he had been with his mother when she actually died. But she had died in the middle of the night. Her bed was empty by the time he got to the hospital. The recovery team from the House of Lazarus had already taken her away. Perhaps he would be less unhappy about her if he had seen her at rest, before she was frozen and stowed away in her drawer.

The bar closed shortly before midnight. Joey mopped the floor. He put the empty bottles in a bin bag and left them out by the back door for the recycling lorry. He said goodnight to Rita.

By this time he had worked out a plan. He knew what he had to do.

He didn't take the bus home. Instead, he took the bus that went across town to the House of Lazarus.

Chapter 6
A Midnight Visit

The receptionist was surprised to see Joey so soon after his last visit. But she remembered his name this time and didn't have to look for it on her computer terminal. After all, he had been here only the day before.

"Your mother will be delighted," the receptionist said. She was glad she had managed to persuade Joey to visit more often. That meant more income for the House of Lazarus. She had done her job well.

An orderly took Joey through to the Wall. It was not the same orderly as yesterday. This one was a man with a pale, sad face. You could easily imagine him working in a funeral parlour. Only his lips moved when he talked. The rest of his face remained completely still, like a mask.

"You know the routine here?" he said.

Joey sat himself down and fitted on the headset. "Yes," he said.

The orderly tapped a command into his hand-held computer. "Then I hope you have a most enjoyable conversation."

"Thank you, I'm sure I will."

The orderly walked away.

Joey looked around him while he waited to hear his mother's voice in the earpiece. There were no more than 30 or 40 visitors at the House of Lazarus at this late hour.

He found the visitor who was sitting closest to one of the doors in the Wall. These were the doors which were marked STAFF ONLY and which you could only open if you knew the code number.

The visitor was an elderly lady. She was having a lovely chat with someone in the Wall, an old friend of hers. She jabbered away, not leaving many pauses for the other person to speak. She was telling her friend about the illnesses she had. "And then there's my hip, which is playing up something awful in this cold weather ..." She seemed to suffer from an awful lot of illnesses.

Joey heard the first muffled murmurings of his mother's voice. He reached for the panel on the armrest and turned down the volume to zero.

"Hello, Mum," he said. "It's me. You can hear me but I can't hear you. I'm sorry about that. I don't want to upset you or anything. You're just going to have to be patient with me. There's something I have to do."

Joey kept talking, as if he was having a conversation. All the while, his attention was on the elderly lady. He was waiting for her to finish. Then she would hit the blue button on her chair, which would bring an orderly.

At last, the elderly lady picked up her handbag and rested it on her lap. She was getting ready to leave. She said goodbye to her friend, then remembered something she had forgotten to mention before. Joey had to hold back a sigh of impatience.

A couple of minutes later the elderly lady said goodbye again. She seemed to mean it this time. Her hand went to the panel. Her finger came down on the blue button.

Joey snatched off his headset and got to his feet.

He was already moving towards the door when an orderly came out to shut down the elderly lady's friend. The orderly gave Joey a polite nod as they passed each other. Joey wanted the orderly to think that he was simply making his way towards the main exit.

Joey got to the door just as it was about to close. He stepped swiftly through the narrow gap.

The door shut with a soft sigh.

Chapter 7
Behind the Wall

Joey found himself in a white corridor. The corridor vibrated with the throb from all the machinery surrounding it. The Wall's stacks of drawers thrummed and hummed overhead.

There was a door at the far end of the corridor. Joey presumed this was where the orderlies went when they weren't helping visitors.

There was also a lift, next to the door.

Joey was almost certain that nobody had spotted him sneaking through the door in the Wall. But he knew he couldn't afford to hang around. He might have been seen, in spite of how careful he had been.

He set off along the corridor at a loping trot. He could scarcely believe he had got this far. He was on the other side of the Wall. The lift would take him upstairs.

He was going to see his mother again!

He pressed the button that would call the lift. The lift was on this floor already. Its heavy, steel doors trundled noisily apart. Joey was just about to enter the lift when the handle turned on the door next to it.

Joey froze in alarm. Then he realised that this was exactly what he mustn't do. Instead, he skipped smartly across the threshold of the lift. At the same moment, someone came out of the room on the other side of the door.

Joey spun round to face the lift's control panel. He slapped the buttons blindly. The lift doors began to come together, but not quickly enough.

A man glanced in. It was the orderly who had attended to Joey a few minutes earlier, the one with the pale, mask-like face. He caught a glimpse of Joey just as the lift doors were almost meeting in the middle. The mask-like face was transformed into a look of complete shock.

"Hey!" he said. "Wait! What are you—?"

The lift doors clunked shut, snipping off the end of the orderly's question.

The lift whirred upwards speedily. Joey saw that its control panel had buttons for three different levels. One was Ground, one was Maintenance and one was Administration. He guessed he needed Maintenance, and by sheer good fortune that was the button he had hit. The button was lit up.

The lift hissed to a halt and the doors opened to reveal a platform that ran alongside the rear of the Wall. The platform was painted white, and so was almost everything else on this side of the Wall, including the Wall itself.

In front of Joey the drawers rose in their stacks, much as they did on the other side. The stacks stretched in both directions as far as the eye could see. The hum of machinery was just as loud, perhaps even louder.

Apart from everything being so white, the main difference here was that there were no armchairs on this side of the Wall. There were huge cranes instead. The cranes were arranged so that they could be guided to every single one of the drawers.

Joey could see a couple of them at work in the distance. They were stately and graceful as they roved up and down the stacks. Their large, metal arms rose and fell like the necks of giant giraffes. Orderlies stood in the cradles at the end of the arms, controlling their movement. The orderlies were running checks on the drawers, making sure they were all working properly. Joey watched them for a while. He couldn't take his eyes off them.

Then the lift doors rolled shut behind him and the lift began to descend. He remembered the orderly who had spotted him getting into the lift on the lower level. No doubt the man had raised the alarm already. Joey realised he had very little time left to do what he wanted to do.

He hurried towards the nearest crane, which was positioned a few metres away along the platform. He clambered over the platform railing and into the crane's cradle.

He examined the controls. He saw an *On* switch and pressed it.

A small display screen lit up and a prompt-message appeared:

STACK NUMBER # ?

The question mark was flashing. Joey turned to the keypad next to the screen and entered the numbers *3*, *3* and *9*. He thought this was the sensible thing to do, and it turned out that it was.

The screen displayed a second prompt-message:

DRAWER NUMBER # ?

Joey put in the numbers *4* and *1*, and all of a sudden the crane began to move.

It extended its arm outwards from the platform, until the cradle was within a few centimetres of the Wall. Then it began to glide sideways along the stacks, heading for Stack 339.

Joey noticed that each drawer was fitted with a rotating handle which was marked off by a ring of black and yellow stripes. He thought that this was so much more convenient than having to dig down through earth and soil. All you had to do was twist and turn the handle, and the drawer would slide open. That was all it would take for him to be able to see his mother again.

Someone on the platform behind him gave a shout. Joey turned his head sharply.

"You!" It was a female orderly, one Joey didn't recognise. She was standing on the platform with an electronic notepad in her hand, looking outraged. "Who are you? You're not qualified to operate that crane."

"I'm going to see my mother," Joey said to her. It sounded crazy and yet, at the same time, very simple.

Just then the lift doors opened and out came three more orderlies. One of them was the man with the mask-like features.

"There he is," he said, pointing at Joey. His face was now creased with lines of unhappiness. Hot, pink circles glowed on his white cheeks. "He's a visitor. He shouldn't be in here."

"Come back here at once," said the orderly with the electronic notepad. She began striding along the platform, trying to catch up with the moving crane and Joey. "You're already in a lot of trouble. Don't make it any worse for yourself."

"I pay to keep her here," Joey said. "I break my back to make enough money to keep her here. So I'll see her if I want to. It's my right."

"But you don't understand," said the orderly. "The drawers have cryogenic seals. You can't open them without breaking the seals. And if you do that, the – er, the physical shock could kill the person inside."

The way the orderly hesitated seemed odd to Joey, as if she wasn't quite convinced by what she was saying.

But it wasn't important, Joey thought. He shook his head calmly.

"I just want to take a look at her," he said. "It'll only be for a moment. Just a quick peek. She'll be fine."

The crane halted abruptly, and Joey had the terrible feeling that it had broken down. Or else maybe the House of Lazarus orderlies had found a way to override the controls. His daring plan seemed to have come to nothing.

Then the crane gave a lurch and started to move again, this time upwards. It had reached Stack 339 and was now climbing to Drawer 41.

"Somebody go and phone Mr Lazarus," said the orderly with the electronic notepad. "Quickly. Quickly!"

There was the clanging of running feet on the platform.

"Please, Mr Newman," begged the orderly with the mask-like face. "Please stop all this. Please stop the crane and come down. I don't think you have any idea what you're doing."

Joey gazed upwards, ignoring him.

"I'm coming, Mum," he said. "I'm coming to see you."

Chapter 8
A Question of Faith

Gordon Lazarus had arrived by the time the orderlies finally managed to bring the crane back down from near the top of Stack 339.

Gordon Lazarus stepped over the railing into the cradle.

Gordon Lazarus spoke to the young man who was lying in a huddle on the floor of the cradle.

"Mr Newman?"

Joey stared straight ahead, his eyes focused on nothing.

"Mr Newman?"

Joey continued to stare.

Then he stirred. He moved his head. He blinked. Finally, in a low, mumbling voice, he said, "Joey. My name's Joey."

"Joey then," said Lazarus. Lazarus reached out a hand. "Come with me, Joey."

Joey took Lazarus's hand. He stood up and allowed himself to be helped out of the crane's cradle and onto the platform. More than a dozen orderlies were now gathered on the platform. The crowd of orderlies parted to let Lazarus and Joey through. Lazarus steered Joey towards the lift. All the while he talked to Joey in soft, soothing tones, the sort of tones you might use when talking to a nervous horse or a frightened child.

Lazarus was wearing the same coal-black suit that he wore in the commercial. The darkness of the suit cloth stood out against the whiteness that was everywhere else. So much whiteness was painful for the eyes. Joey found it restful to look at Lazarus's suit.

The lift carried them up to the Administration level. Lazarus led Joey along a corridor to an office. It looked nothing like the office in the commercial. This one was modern and practical. The furniture was made of plastic and steel, and there was the very latest model of computer on the desk. There were no pictures on the walls, and no bust of a Roman emperor.

Lazarus made Joey sit down and asked if he would like a drink. Joey didn't say yes or no, so Lazarus poured him one anyway. He placed the tumbler full of whisky in Joey's shaking hand. Lazarus poured himself a

drink, too, and sat on the edge of the desk.
He took a sip, then began talking.

First of all he talked about faith. He said
that faith was necessary in all areas of life.
Faith was what made humans the wonderful
creatures they were. Civilisation would fall
apart if people didn't have faith in one
another and in a higher power. There was an
old saying about love making the world go
round, but Lazarus said he thought it was
faith that made the world go round. Faith was
trusting in everyone else to do what they
believed was right. Faith was knowing that
there was more to life than meets the eye.

Then he started talking about how
difficult it was to make cryogenics work.
It was impossible for bodies to survive for
very long, even in subzero conditions.
Cells began to break down. Organs began to
decay. You just couldn't keep bodies
preserved in ice for ever.

Then he started using a whole string of complex, technical terms. He said things like *neural network* and *connection modules* and *quantum software*.

This would not have meant much to Joey before tonight. However, he had seen what was in the drawer that was supposed to contain his mother's body. So now he knew what Lazarus was referring to.

"Artificial intelligence," he said.

"You could call it that," said Lazarus, nodding. "We prefer to call it 'real-time character interface'. You remember those tests we ran on your mother? The interviews we conducted?"

"The salesman said you were recording her voice for sampling."

"We were. But what we were also doing was building up a picture of your mother's personality. We learned how her mind

73

worked, how she reacted to certain questions. We learned what words she liked to use, certain sayings she was fond of, things like that. And we programmed it all into a hard drive in order to create a perfect computerised copy of your mother. The copy can respond to you, and develop lines of conversation with you. It even knows what's on the news. It's as good as actually having your mother there."

"She was just wires and disks and chipboards."

"But she's *real*, isn't she, Joey?" Lazarus said, with a glint in his eye. "She's *real* to you. That's what counts."

Joey couldn't deny the truth in this. She *had* seemed real. Until now, he had been in no doubt that what lay in Drawer 41 in Stack 339 was his mother.

"What did you do with her body?" he asked.

"Your mother was cremated," Lazarus replied. "We have a private crematorium here and we employ a priest full-time to oversee the funeral service. We gave her a proper send-off. You see, I'm not a monster, Joey. You may be thinking right now that I am, but I'm not. I have a profound respect for the dead. After all, I'm going to be dead myself one of these days."

Joey stared hard at him.

Lazarus stared back.

"However, I'm also a man who can't afford to take risks," Lazarus said. "I can't afford for the public to know what really goes on here at the House of Lazarus. That would not be good for business. Not good for business at all. So I need to know something from you, Joey. I need to know what you're going to do about this. I need to know how you're going to deal with what you've found out tonight."

Joey thought hard. He could go to the police. He could go to a newspaper. He could expose the House of Lazarus and the whole place would be shut down.

However, he had a strong feeling that Gordon Lazarus would not allow that to happen. He could tell this by the way Lazarus was staring at him. He thought about the private crematorium Lazarus had just mentioned. It would be an easy way to dispose of the bodies of people who could cause you problems. Perhaps that was another reason why Lazarus had mentioned it.

Could Lazarus be so ruthless? Would he be prepared to resort to murder just to keep the secret of the House of Lazarus safe? Joey reckoned he would.

"I don't know," Joey said. "I need some time to think."

Lazarus glanced at his watch. He looked as if he was considering whether he could give Joey the time he needed. Then he shook his head. "That's just not possible, Joey. What is possible, though, is that you can accept the offer which I'm about to make."

"Offer?" said Joey.

"Yes. It's a very generous offer, too."

Lazarus explained what his offer was. It did seem very generous.

"But I have to have an answer from you straight away," Lazarus added. "I have to know what you're going to do so that I know what I'm going to do."

Joey remembered the contestant on *Lose Everything*. Like her, his whole future depended on what he said next. He could win the star prize if he gave the correct answer ... or he could lose everything.

Chapter 9
The Privileged Visitor

"Hello, Joey. How good to see you again," said the receptionist.

Joey was a regular visitor to the House of Lazarus these days and felt that the receptionist's smile was no longer false. She saw him so often that she had become quite fond of him.

It helped that he had "privileged visitor" status nowadays. This meant that he got to speak to his mother whenever he wanted to, for free, and didn't have to pay rent for her drawer any longer. The receptionist seemed to have a greater respect for him because of this.

"Go on through," she said.

The Wall had become a familiar sight. Joey was no longer impressed by it. But he liked the coldness in the air. He liked the fact that it was all faked to make people think that there really were bodies on ice in those drawers. It was a trick. The House of Lazarus was just giving you what you expected. He admired that, in a way.

Stack 339, Drawer 41 was still where his mother lay.

Joey picked up the headset microphone. "Mum?" he said. He told her everything he had done today and everything he planned to do tomorrow.

"I'll be moving soon. I've saved up enough for the down payment on a new place. There's a flat in Fisherman's Reach that I like the look of."

He was getting his life sorted at last.

"I'm still hunting around for another job. I've got a couple of interviews. But you'll be glad to hear that I'm not working at the bar any more."

Joey didn't have to lie to her any more, and that was a relief.

"And Mum, I've met someone. You'd like her. Her name's Kelly. I'll bring her along sometime so you can meet her. I'm happy now, Mum. Honestly I am."

All along, he had needed his mother, without realising how much he had needed her.

He hadn't wanted her to die any more than she herself had wanted to die.

And he had faith in the House of Lazarus.

"And you sound happy too, Mum. I'm glad about that. Very glad," Joey went on.

He had faith in the illusion which Gordon Lazarus had created.

It was a glorious illusion.

Wasn't it?

Barrington Stoke would like to thank all its readers for commenting on the manuscript before publication and in particular:

Iona Anderson
Ellie Bate
Laurie Burns
Sarah Crane
Kim Donohoe
Paul Duncan
Suzanne Graham
Eilidh Harper
Claire Kennedy
Naomi Krug

Sophie Lambrakis
Tom Larsen
Sarah Lawrence
Andrew Lewis
Kirsty McCaskill
Iain McColl
Abi Rose
Jafar Hmzah Tiyar
Josie Vallely

Become a Consultant!

Would you like to give us feedback on our titles before they are published? Contact us at the address below – we'd love to hear from you!

Barrington Stoke, 10 Belford Terrace, Edinburgh EH4 3DQ
Tel: 0131 315 4933 Fax: 0131 315 4934
E-mail: info@barringtonstoke.co.uk
Website: www.barringtonstoke.co.uk

More Teen Titles!

Joe's Story by Rachel Anderson 1-902260-70-8
Playing Against the Odds by Bernard Ashley 1-902260-69-4
Harpies by David Belbin 1-842990-31-4
Firebug by Eric Brown 1-842991-03-5
TWOCKING by Eric Brown 1-842990-42-X
To Be A Millionaire by Yvonne Coppard 1-902260-58-9
All We Know of Heaven by Peter Crowther 1-842990-32-2
Walking with Rainbows by Isla Dewar 1-842991-30-2
The Ring of Truth by Alan Durant 1-842990-33-0
Falling Awake by Viv French 1-902260-54-6
The Wedding Present by Adèle Geras 1-902260-77-5
The Cold Heart of Summer by Alan Gibbons 1-842990-80-2
Before Night Falls by Keith Gray 1-842991-24-8
The Shadow on the Stairs by Ann Halam 1-902260-57-0
Alien Deeps by Douglas Hill 1-902260-55-4
Partners in Crime by Nigel Hinton 1-842991-02-7
The New Girl by Mary Hooper 1-842991-01-9
Dade County's Big Summer by Lesley Howarth 1-842990-43-8
Runaway Teacher by Pete Johnson 1-902260-59-7
No Stone Unturned by Brian Keaney 1-842990-34-9
Wings by James Lovegrove 1-842990-11-X
A Kind of Magic by Catherine MacPhail 1-842990-10-1
Stalker by Anthony Masters 1-842990-81-0
Clone Zone by Jonathan Meres 1-842990-09-8
The Dogs by Mark Morris 1-902260-76-7
Turnaround by Alison Prince 1-842990-44-6
Dream On by Bali Rai 1-842990-45-4
What's Your Problem? by Bali Rai 1-842991-26-4
All Change by Rosie Rushton 1-902260-75-9
Fall Out by Rosie Rushton 1-842990-74-8
The Blessed and The Damned by Sara Sheridan 1-842990-08-X
Double Vision by Norman Silver 1-842991-00-0